The Planet of Doom...

When the inhabitants fled their home in despair, thundering through the skies in immense silver starships, they left behind cities already crumbling in decay. It would not take long for those once-majestic structures to become ruins, half covered in vegetation or buried in creeping sands. The people took care, however, to leave behind one high-powered radio beacon. Its message, designed to repeat endlessly for centuries to come, would caution any approaching ship to stay away from the abandoned world with its deadly contagion. *DANGER! DANGER!* the beacon warned, piercing the planet's tainted atmosphere to pass far out into the void of interstellar space.

Unfortunately, the scout ship from Earth which arrived a thousand years later did not quite understand the message.

"At last!" the ship's captain exclaimed in delight and excitement to her crew as the coded message came through the com. "After all these centuries, someone is finally sending us an invitation!"

TALES FROM THE WONDER ZONE

Stardust
·
Explorer
·
Orbiter

More Science Fiction
from Trifolium Books Inc.

**Packing Fraction
& Other Tales of Science
and Imagination**

Stardust

Edited by
Julie E. Czerneda

Illustrated by
Jean-Pierre Normand

Trifolium Books Inc.
Toronto, Canada

We acknowledge the financial support of the Government of Canada through
the Book Publishing Industry Development Program (BPIDP) for our publishing
activities.

Canadian Cataloguing in Publication Data
Main entry under title: Stardust
(Tales from the wonder zone)
ISBN 1-55244-018-4

1. Children's stories, Canadian (English).* 2. Children's stories, American.
3. Science fiction, Canadian (English).* 4. Science fiction, American.
I. Czerneda, Julie E., 1955–   . II. Normand, Jean-Pierre. III. Series.

PS8323.S3S72 2002   ¡813'.08762089282   C00-931742-2
PZ5.S733 2002

Trifolium Books Inc.
250 Merton Street, Suite 203,
Toronto Ontario M4S 1B1
info@trifoliumbooks.com   www.trifoliumbooks.com

Cover Design and Illustrations: Jean-Pierre Normand
Text Design: John Lee, Heidy Lawrance Associates

Printed in Canada
9 8 7 6 5 4 3 2 1

Dedications

Julie E. Czerneda: To Jim Rogerson, who envisioned this series and insisted it be gorgeous. To all the contributors, for having wonder in their pockets. To Gregory Benford, with special thanks for his introduction to this book. And to Jean-Pierre, who put his heart and soul, as well as talent, into every piece of art.

Jean-Pierre Normand: To my parents, Marcel Normand and Bernadette Morin, who made it all possible for me.

Annette Griessman: For Alex and Kayla with love. And a special thanks to Julie for her faith in me.

Mark Leslie: Special thank you to Francine Marzanek, for insight into scientific principles, guidance, and support.

Alison Baird: For Jay, a true original.

James Van Pelt: To his three sons, Dylan, Samuel, and Joshua, who heard the story first.

Beverley J. Meincke: To Julie Czerneda, for having faith in me when I had none in myself. For taking me under her wing and teaching me to fly.

CONTENTS

A Special Introduction by Gregory Benford

You hold in your hands a book of wonder. These stories are not mere dreams, though. They rely on real knowledge, solid science.

They promise the sense of reality, but they are stories, not lectures. This is a tradition that goes far back, all the way to the legendary French writer, Jules Verne. By telling you a few of the ways Verne thought about his time — as long ago now as the American Civil War — perhaps one can see how a savvy pursuit of wonder can be the most wonderful route to a future that will be different.

In 1865, there were six interplanetary adventure books published in French, with titles like *Voyage to Venus, An Inhabitant of the Planet Mars, Voyage to the Moon,* and even a survey by an astronomer, *Imaginary Moons and Real Moons.* They featured balloons as a means of travel in space. One writer did have a dim idea of using rockets — but his squirted water out the end, not fiery gas. He ruined the effect, though, by thriftily collecting the ejected water to use again. Elementary common sense should have told him that such a ship would gain no momentum that way. The water's push would be cancelled when the water was caught.

Verne made fun of this invention, saying that his own method, a cannon, would certainly work. (The idea of the squirter that recycles its water had a puzzling appeal; it was proposed by an engineer as recently as 1927.) You see, when Verne wrote about going to the moon, he *dreamed exactly*. That's what gave his work the headlong confidence those other volumes of 1865 lacked.

Verne's story gave many of the telling little details which now strike us as so right. Since the USA was the most likely nation of his time to undertake so bold a venture, that was where his veterans placed their cannon. Where in the USA? Verne talked about getting into the right "plane of the ecliptic," which is a reasonable motivation, but sidesteps the more detailed issue. He knew that to artillery gunners, Earth's rotation was important in predicting where a shell would land — while a shell is flying through the air, the land moves beneath it.

In aiming for the moon, there's an even bigger effect. Think of the Earth as a huge merry-go-round. If you stand at the North Pole, the Earth spins under your feet, but you won't move at all. Stand on the equator, though, and the Earth swings you around at a speed of about a thousand miles an hour. You don't feel it, because the air is moving, too.

But that speed matters a lot if you're aiming to leap into orbit. Verne had the crucial idea right — that *escape velocity* is the essential factor in getting away from Earth's gravitational pull. The added boost from the Earth's rotation led him to believe that the American adventurers would seek a spot as close to the equator as possible, while still keeping it within their nation. A glance at the map told him that the obvious sites were in Texas or Florida.

This is exactly what happened in the American space program of nearly a century later, when the launch site of the Apollo program became a political football between Texas and Florida. Florida won, as Verne predicted. Not for political reasons, though. NASA engineers wanted their rocket stages to fall harmlessly into the ocean. Verne even picked Stone Hill, on almost the exact latitude as Cape Kennedy, the Apollo program's launch site.

Similarly, Verne correctly described the shape of the capsule, the number of astronauts (three), weightlessness in space, a splashdown at sea picked up by the Navy, and even the use of rockets to change orbit and return to Earth.

To give his technology authority, his characters were described as cool dudes of geometry: "Here and there he wrote a pi or an x^2. He even appeared to extract a certain cube root with the greatest of ease." Even if Verne didn't always get the math right, still he had the mannerisms, the lingo. And what dreams Verne had! We can grasp how much he changed the world by recalling real events, which appeared first as acts of imagination in his novels.

Consider: The American submarine *Nautilus* had its name taken from the Jules Verne novel, *20,000 Leagues under the Sea*. Like the submarine in Verne's book, this *Nautilus* surfaced at the North Pole and talked by radio with the President of the United States, less than a century after the novel was published. The explorer Haroun Tazieff, a Verne fan who had read *Journey to the Center of the Earth*, climbed down into the rumbling throat of a volcano in Africa, seeking secrets of the Earth's core. An Italian adventurer coasted over the icy Arctic wastes in a dirigible, just as Verne proposed. A French explorer crawled into the caves of southern Europe, stumbling upon the ancient campgrounds of early man, standing before underground lakes where mammoths once roasted over crackling fires — as Verne had envisioned decades before. In 1877, Verne foresaw a journey through the entire solar system, a feat accomplished by NASA's robot voyagers a century later.

And so the stories in this book may very well give us images of what will be, of wonders to come. Or, to be truthful, maybe not. The aim of science fiction, even of the kind most honest with the facts, is not to predict the future. Instead, such stories try to influence the future. They try to guide us toward or away from possibilities.

But to do so, the authors have to know their stuff. Not only do they need to be clever enough to avoid making obvious mistakes, as well, they must choose the science and engineering background to open our eyes.

These stories of wonder envision how the science we know today could play out on the stage of our future. In the end, their most powerful effect will come when *you* take their ideas

into your own mind and play with them, making a future of your own. For even though fiction helps shape us, in the end it is we who shape the future.

Gregory Benford

Dr. Gregory Benford is a professor of physics at the University of California, Irvine, and the author of *Jupiter Project* and *Eater*.

Alien Games

by Annette Griessman

Andris closed one eye and carefully tossed the shiny metal ball toward the first of three triangles he had drawn in the dirt. The ball fell short and hit one of his sister's clear, crystal balls. It bounced off and rolled out across the open ground. Andris frowned at the horrible shot. He would never get the hang of playing slicer here in the heavier gravity of Tycha. Chandra, on the other hand, seemed to actually play better here than on Earth — she had won four straight games. Andris glanced at her. Her expression was carefully blank, but Andris knew her well enough to see the twinkle in her eye. He sighed. At least she had stopped openly gloating.

1

Chandra turned toward Andris' ball. It had stopped right in front of two imposing looking guards. "Be careful," she warned. "Your ball almost went into the village."

Andris bent down to pick up a second ball. He rolled it between his fingers, enjoying its cool smoothness. This was his best slicer ball and he never missed with it. It was time for him to win one of these stupid games. He patiently watched as Chandra moved over to retrieve his first ball. The Tychan guards paid no attention. They stood like statues, their emerald eyes trained in an unblinking stare at a point just in front of their orange-hued faces. One guard's grass-colored hair blew into his eye, but he made no move to brush it away. They stood there like that all day, supposedly guarding the Tychan village from evil spirits. It was the most ridiculous thing Andris had ever seen.

"So what are the carrot-heads going to do if I cross the line? Arrest me?" Andris shook his head in disgust. "We've been here almost six months, and they are still trying to figure out if we're civilized! We land here in space ships, build our camp out of boxes with high-tech tools, and they don't know if *we're* civilized." He nodded toward one of the guards. "*They're* the ones who guard against evil spirits, not us."

Chandra's face took on that annoyed, tight-lipped look that meant she was going to lecture him. He held up a hand to stop her. "I know. Different planet. Different culture. I know the drill."

Chandra's expression softened. "I was going to say you shouldn't call them carrot-heads." She glanced back toward the village where their dad, Major Frank Simms, was walking toward the village meeting hall with the Tychan leader, U'mola. The two were chatting together in a friendly way, their dad's face creased in a smile and U'mola's hands waving up and down in a Tychan expression of pleasure. But Andris and Chandra were both aware of the tension beneath the friendliness. Their dad's job was to negotiate for colony land rights for Earth to set up a permanent farming community. The Tychans, on the other hand, had no interest in talking about land — they hadn't decided yet whether humans were civilized beings, or if they were little more than well-trained animals. The problem was, no one in the human camp could really figure out what the Tychans considered *civilized*. Their language and culture were difficult to understand.

Andris focused his attention back on the game. The whole situation made him mad. If his dad couldn't negotiate land rights here, then soon all of them would have to leave and try to establish a farming colony on Omega Prime. The fact was, Earth needed food that a farming colony could provide, no matter where it was. But Andris liked it here. The weather was warm and the sea was calm

5

with a wide, red beach. Omega Prime was a jungle world — hot, humid, and full of very large bugs. Andris *hated* bugs.

He pushed his anger aside, took a deep breath, and closed one eye. All that mattered at this moment was knocking his sister's ball from the first triangle. Negotiating for the land for the colony was out of his hands.

He threw just a bit harder this time, to try and make up for the heavy gravity. He grimaced as the ball left his hand and sailed through the air. Maybe too hard, he thought. The ball hit the ground and rolled and rolled… right past the two guards and onto the village's main road. The road's surface was black and slick, as slick as ice, his dad said, and the ball rolled even farther. It stopped against the wall of the meeting hall. *Argh!* Way too hard!

The guards kept their gaze steady. Chandra bit back a gasp. And Andris shook his head and started out after his ball.

"H-hey!" sputtered Chandra. "Where are you going?"

Andris pointed. "What's it look like? That's my favorite slicer ball!"

Chandra leaned out and snagged his arm, her expression one of panic. "You can't *do* that, Andris! The village is off limits until the Tychans say we're civilized. You could get Dad in big trouble!"

Andris reluctantly stopped. He eyed his ball — it was so close! He eyed the two guards, considering.

Would they stop him, he wondered? Or would they just stare into space like they always did? It's not like he was an evil spirit or anything. He felt his frown return. Chandra did have a point, though. If he went into the village, and the Tychans got upset, then his dad would be the one in trouble, not him. He didn't want that.

His jaw tightened angrily. But he also wanted his slicer ball.

As he stared at the distant metal ball, it seemed to wink at him, reflecting the light of the orange Tychan sun. It seemed to be urging him to march into the village, pick it up, and proclaim to all the carrot-heads that he, Andris Simms, was civilized because he never lost a slicer ball. It made him so mad he could hardly stand it. Before he could follow his instinct to go get his ball, he turned and stomped across the clearing. He slumped down next to his littlest sister, Kellin.

Chandra followed and sat beside him. She crossed her arms and sighed. "Now, what? You want to play something else?" She idly leaned over and picked up Kellin's toy, a bright pink bug that crawled across the sand. She turned it to face her and smiled at its wide, goofy grin and bobbing antennae. Kellin had been running the bug in a figure-eight pattern to practice controlling it with the bright purple controller. It still tried to crawl while in Chandra's hand, its six legs waving.

7

"Hey, put that down!" said Kellin, with a toss of her pigtails. "I'm just getting good."

Chandra smiled and plopped the bug down. It resumed its slow, steady walk, stepping on Andris' foot in the process. It bobbled a bit, but kept right on going. Andris rolled his eyes. Too bad the stupid bug couldn't go over and get his slicer ball. Maybe the Tychans would think *it* was civilized.

Andris blinked. He looked at the silly pink bug. His forehead creased as he watched it go. *Chunk! Chunk! Chunk!* Out over the sand it went, getting good traction with its rounded metal feet on the uneven surface. If that bug had hands, maybe it *could* pick up his ball. He licked his lips as he considered the possibilities.

Andris grinned and jumped up. He had an idea... a daring and wild idea. One that just might work. He turned and raced for the squat supply building of the temporary colony.

In only a short time, he was back, a large box in hand. He sat the box down and began rummaging around in its depths.

Chandra and Kellin watched in silence as he carefully placed a small motor, a remote switch, a long metal bar, and two tiny pulleys on the ground. "Where'd you get all that stuff?" asked Chandra finally.

"The Shipmaster's tool box," muttered Andris, his hands busy.

Chandra's eyes widened. "Are you *crazy?* No one messes with the Shipmaster's toolbox. If he catches you, he'll make you polish the whole space ship with a toothbrush!"

"Only if he catches me," said Andris. He picked up Kellin's crawling bug. "Can I borrow this, Kellin?"

Kellin glared at him. "What for?"

"I'm going to use it to get my slicer ball back." Kellin's expression didn't change. Andris tried again. "I promise I won't hurt it, okay? Please?"

Kellin's eyes narrowed. "Only if you give me your ice cream tonight."

Andris nodded. "Done." He pulled an adhesive patch from the box and carefully fastened the small motor to the top of the grinning bug, waving a light pen back and forth across the seal. The blue light activated the adhesive, which would then stick tight to almost any surface. A flick of a switch and the light from the pen could be changed to white, which would just as easily remove the adhesive. Kellin's bug would remain undamaged.

Once the motor was attached, he pulled a tiny controller from the box and toggled a switch on it. The motor started up smoothly, the tiny shaft sticking from its side spinning just as it should. Andris used the controller to turn it off. He then attached the thin metal rod next to the motor and slid one tiny pulley down to its base. The pulley was fastened to the motor's shaft so it would spin when the motor was

9

turned on. Andris fastened the second pulley to the top of the rod, and tied a string between them. He sat back on his heels to admire his creation.

Chandra had moved closer to better see what he was doing. "I get it. You're going to send the bug into the village, turn on the motor with the remote, have the string reel out, and snag the ball. Right?"

"Right," said Andris. "I just need something at the end of the string to grab hold of the ball. Glue or adhesive or..." He waved his hand in exasperation. He wasn't sure what to put at the end of the string. "... or something."

Chandra made a strange face and reached into her pocket. She pulled out a small, black disc. "Will this do?"

Andris stared. "A magnet? Why do you have a magnet in your pocket?"

The corners of Chandra's mouth twitched and her eyes twinkled. "I cheat at slicer." When Andris only blinked at her, she added, "You know... you use *metal* balls. The magnet is useful to... well... adjust some of the goal shots."

Andris rolled his eyes. She cheated! No wonder he couldn't win a game! He snatched the magnet from her hand. "We'll have a rematch later — and I'll make sure you can't *adjust* any shots."

Kellin giggled and Chandra grinned as Andris fastened the magnet to the end of the string. He gently placed the bug on the ground, ready to send it on its way.

"Oh, wait!" exclaimed Chandra, rummaging through the box. "What about the road?"

"What about it?" asked Andris, squinting at its slick, black surface.

"The bug's metal feet will slip on that. Do you have some rubber...something to give it a better grip?"

Andris realized Chandra was right...the bug would slide around on the road. And then he might not get his slicer ball back. But he didn't have anything to put onto the bug's feet to help it get better traction.

"How about these?" Kellin held up two rubbery hair bands, her hair now loose around her face.

"Yeah! We can fasten pieces of those to the bug's feet. That will work!" said Chandra, now thoroughly involved in the job of retrieving Andris' ball.

Andris glanced at Kellin. "How much?"

Kellin gave him a sly look. "Your ice cream for the rest of the week."

Andris grimaced. "You're pushing it, Kellin. But okay." He took the bands and he and Chandra cut them with a tool from the box and stuck them to the bug's feet with more adhesive.

"Now?" asked Andris, giving both his sisters a look.

"Now," they agreed, nodding.

Andris took the purple controller from Kellin and sent the bug on its way.

It crawled across the ground at a snail's pace. Andris wished it went faster. He bit his lip and tried to be patient. It crossed over the first slicer triangle... across the second...and then across the third. It crept on tiny legs toward the two passive guards.

Andris was now on his feet, Chandra at his elbow. Kellin hung off to one side. They all breathlessly waited expectantly to see what would happen when the bug crossed the village boundary.

The bug marched past the two guards' feet, without them giving it a second glance.

"Wow," breathed Chandra. "I guess it doesn't count as an evil spirit."

"Guess not," mumbled Andris, turning the controller's knob to keep the bug on course. "Or maybe they've learned to sleep with their eyes open."

Chandra snorted and fell silent. They watched the bug step up onto the road. It slipped a bit, then trudged out across the black surface. On toward the meeting hall, and on toward the slicer ball.

Andris stopped the bug just in front of the metal ball. He set the purple controller down and picked up the smaller one that controlled the motor switch. He squinted. He couldn't see well enough from this distance. He moved closer, stopping just past the

12

third slicer triangle. Chandra was right behind him, holding tightly to Kellin's hand. They were close to the carrot-headed guards, and their impassive green stares made Andris a little nervous. His fingers trembled slightly as he toggled the switch to turn the motor on.

The string slowly lowered. Andris held his breath as the magnet settled on the ground, only a centimeter from the ball. "Come on...come on!" he muttered. The ball stayed still for a long moment, then it began to roll. It settled onto the magnet with a satisfying *clink!*

"Yes!" exclaimed Andris. He toggled the switch. The string reeled back up, taking the ball with it. Then he grabbed the purple controller and started the bug back the way it had come.

He was so occupied with his task that he didn't notice the two small figures that watched from beside the building. First one, then the other, crept out onto the road, their green eyes bright with curiosity.

"Uh...Andris?" Chandra tugged at his sleeve.

"What?" He was having trouble turning the bug. Its antennae bobbed wildly as it bounced over a rock. It kept on going, its goofy grin never fading.

"You're attracting attention."

Andris glanced to where she pointed. The two Tychan children were closer now, both bent over, peering this way and that at the strange invader.

Andris' eyes darted to the meeting hall. He recognized the Tychan kids. They were U'mola's own children. They would tell her about the crawling pink bug for sure. Andris turned the controller knob and tried to turn the bug faster. Maybe if he got the thing out of there, everything would be okay...

...the bug turned sharply and ran straight into a rock. Andris, Chandra, and Kellin all gasped as it teetered on two legs...and slowly toppled over.

One of the Tychan children reached down, flicked his hand in a strange gesture, and then picked it up. The pink contrasted oddly with the child's orange-toned skin. The two small Tychans looked at each other, and then ran, bug and all, into the meeting hall.

"No! Wait!" yelled Andris. Without thinking, he rushed forward. He slid with difficulty to a stop on the slick road. His mouth fell open and his heart raced in panic as he realized he now stood just outside the meeting hall. Past the guards and past the village boundary.

He spun around. The two guards had definitely noticed his passage. They had both turned and now gazed at him, their faces blank. Andris looked from one to the other, and tried to figure out if he could make it back past them before they grabbed him. Chandra and Kellin stared at him, their eyes wide.

"Uh...uh... I didn't mean it," whispered Andris,

inching back toward the village boundary. "Honest I didn't..."

"What's going on here?" demanded a familiar voice from behind him. Andris spun again, almost falling on the slick road, to face his dad.

"Uh...Dad! Nothing, really. I just lost my slicer ball and I didn't want to cross into the village and so we fixed Kellin's bug to get it but it fell over and the two kids grabbed it and I ran..." Andris stopped his rapid speech as his dad's expression darkened. *I'm in big trouble now,* he thought, and closed his mouth with a snap. Nothing he could say would get him out of this mess.

His dad took a deep breath. The shouting was about to begin. Andris fought the urge to cover his ears. But before his dad could let loose, a soft, musical voice interrupted.

"What is this beautiful thing?" U'mola stepped out of the hall, her accent barely noticeable as she carefully pronounced her newly learned English words. She held up the bright pink bug. Two bright-eyed children clung to her skirts.

Major Simms, all business now, looked at his son. "Why don't you tell her?"

Andris gulped and blinked back tears as he turned to U'mola. "I lost my slicer ball." Her head tilted as she regarded him curiously.

"Slicer? Ball?"

Andris nodded. "Slicer's a game. And I lost my ball, you see." He forced himself to look straight into her deep green eyes. "I didn't want to cross into the village, so we fixed Kellin's toy," he pointed at the bug, "to come in and pick it up. But then..." Andris trailed off, remembering how he had rushed headlong into the village.

U'mola blinked and waited.

"...then, when your children picked up the bug, I rushed after it." He tried to put his feelings into his face and voice so she wouldn't be mad. "I really am sorry."

U'mola blinked again. Major Simms shifted uncomfortably. Andris wished he could sink into the ground. Now they would never have a colony here, he was sure of it. And it was all because of him.

"You humans play games?" U'mola's gaze was steady, calm.

Andris nodded. "Uh, yeah. Lots of them."

U'mola's hand flicked. Andris wasn't sure if it was a gesture of pleasure or disgust. "And you did not wish to dishonor your father or us by crossing the boundary. Even to get your...slicer...ball?" she said the words carefully.

"Yes," Andris frowned slightly. U'mola's reaction wasn't what he'd expected.

"And so you sent this thing of beauty instead." It wasn't a question, but a statement of fact.

18

Andris gulped nervously. "Yes."

U'mola's hand flicked again. Behind her, her children's hands flicked as well. "Your name, child?"

"Andris, ma'am. Andris Simms."

U'mola glanced at Major Simms, then turned back to Andris. Her lips curled slightly as she attempted to copy a human smile. "Then, Andris, you are most civilized. You are welcome in our village anytime."

Andris gaped in surprise. "I *am?*"

"He *is?*" gasped Andris' dad. "But what makes him, pardon me for asking...civilized?"

Both of U'mola's hands flicked, in what Andris was now sure, meant pleasure. "He lost a part of his *game*, Major Simms. To the Tychan people, nothing is more civilized than a good game." She grasped the shiny metal ball, still swinging from the magnet, and plucked it off. She handed it gently to Andris. "This game ball is a most important thing. And for such a thing, he didn't wish to dishonor our village. That consideration is also the mark of one who is civilized."

Andris' father was speechless. Andris knew him well enough to know what he was thinking. Six months of talking...when they should have been playing games.

"Well, then," the major said finally. "How would you like to learn to play baseball? That's one of our best games."

19

U'mola nodded, but looked at Andris. "I would like that very much, Major Simms. We can learn that later as you build your farming colony. But first, I would like to learn to play this *slicer*." Her lips curved wider. "Would you mind showing me, young Andris?"

Andris smiled slowly. They would allow the colony after all. And all because of a game. "I would love to." He flicked his own hand in imitation of U'mola's gesture of pleasure. She nodded and gently took that hand. Together, they walked past the guards to the slicer triangles. Chandra and Kellin smiled shyly as they approached.

Andris gave Chandra a look. This time, he thought, he would make sure she didn't cheat.

Looking Through Glass

by Mark Leslie

"**S**omeone's been sneaking in here and stealing my ideas," Uncle Zak had told Paul on his last weekly visit to the scientist's house. Those very words rang in Paul's ears as he stood on the front step to Uncle Zak's house and spied, through the front window, a long dark shadow moving along the wall.

Paul stepped closer to the edge of the step so that he could better see the figure lurking on the other side of the window. As he got close enough to peer inside, he caught sight of a tall gangly man standing in the middle of the room. The man was hefting a brick toward the window.

Paul ducked, covering his eyes as the sound of shattering glass filled the air. "Hey!" he shouted, feeling tiny fragments of the broken window landing in his hair and bouncing off his face. "What gives?"

Uncle Zak was leaning his tall, gangly frame out the window muttering apologies as Paul felt cool liquid running down his forehead and face in several spots. "So sorry, Paul. I didn't realize anyone was there." Paul brought a hand up to the liquid streaming down his face, thinking he'd been cut in multiple locations and wondering why his blood felt so cold.

"Uncle Zak. What's going on? Why is my blood cold and clear?"

Uncle Zak laughed and almost fell out the window. "Paul, my dear nephew. You're not bleeding at all."

"But… the glass."

"It's not regular glass. It's a special mixture I've developed. Taste it."

Paul ran a hand along the liquid streaming down his face, then licked his fingers. "Hey. It tastes like water."

"That's because it *is* mostly water. The door is open. C'mon in and I'll explain."

Still running a hand through his hair, checking for bleeding, Paul opened the front door and stepped inside. He made his way down the short front hallway and turned right at the first doorway — the doorway to Uncle Zak's laboratory. As he walked, Paul mused about the tastefully decorated home and the lab which could be mistaken for a reading room or den if not for the presence of a sink, some flasks, Bunsen burners, and other lab-like fixtures.

When Paul was younger and didn't know his uncle Zakariah Debizynchik very well, he used to imagine that his uncle's entire house was filled with test tubes, pots of strange boiling liquids, jars with exotic contents like an eyeball or perhaps the heart of a dead cow; and maybe, just maybe, in a dark corner of one room, a tall, stiff, motionless body with bolts coming out of its neck could be spotted, waiting for the next lightning storm to bring it to life.

But Uncle Zak's place wasn't anything like the labs of mad professors Paul had seen in movies or read about in comic books. And Uncle Zak himself wasn't anything like the professors in those same stories, either. In fact, Uncle Zak was a man who loved to spend time with others, and particularly enjoyed a good laugh. He made a point of extending a weekly invitation to Paul to come for a visit, especially after he'd learned that his grades in Science were slipping. But Uncle Zak didn't just talk about science and technology with his nephew; he told him jokes, stories, and they sometimes watched movies together or went out to the local arcade — and somewhere in all that fun, Uncle Zak always managed to teach Paul something new about the world of science. And since those weekly visits began, Paul's grades started to creep back up again.

When Paul walked into the lab, Uncle Zak was crouched on the floor near the window. "Some of the broken glass fell on the floor in here. Would you mind helping me clean it up?"

"Sure," Paul said as he walked over to the utility cabinet to grab the broom and dustpan.

"You won't need those," Uncle Zak said without looking up. "Grab that roll of paper towels off my desk."

Paul took the paper towels and walked over to his uncle. Looking at the floor as he handed Uncle Zak the paper towels, he didn't spot any shiny fragments of glass at all. Instead there were little pools of water on the hardwood floor. With the paper towel, Uncle Zak wiped up the tiny droplets. Then he stood up, turned, and smiled at his nephew.

"Bet you never imagined cleaning up a broken window would be this easy."

Paul shook his head, still not understanding what was going on.

"Now that that's done, how would you like to help me replace the broken pane?"

"Sure." Paul said. "Do you have a new one here or will we have to go to the hardware store?"

"Neither." Uncle Zak smiled a wide-toothed smile and hooked a thumb in the direction of the window. "See that green button on the window frame over there? Just go and press it."

Seeing the green button, just above a red one on the right side of the window frame, Paul walked over and pressed it.

A hum sounded, not unlike the hum of a fluorescent light, and the edges of the frame glowed slightly, then, after a few more seconds, there was a frame of what looked like glass in the previously paneless window. Paul reached out and touched it. It felt cool, but was solid.

"How did you make this? How is this possible?" Paul asked, his jaw hanging down.

Uncle Zak smiled again, let out a short laugh, and then spoke. "It's a frozen water compound. Regular tap water, some chlorine, and a few other chemicals. Essentially, the window pane is made up of a very thin layer of clear ice. The window frame is really where I put all the work. You see, the frame creates an extremely focused area about one centimeter thick that can maintain a consistent temperature. In this case, it's approximately zero degrees Celsius. When you press the green button, a thin layer of water drops out of the top of the frame and into this temperature core, freezing into a fine sheet of ice."

Paul looked at the window. It seemed like a normal window. "But ice isn't usually so clear. Isn't it usually fuzzy and bumpy?"

"When formed naturally, ice usually is all fuzzy and bumpy," his Uncle agreed, "depending on where it's frozen and how long it takes to freeze. Chemicals like chlorine and other ones I've added that are a little harder to pronounce, kind of like my full name, help keep the ice clear and clean. And the fact that it's less than a centimeter thick also helps assure that the light coming through the ice doesn't refract so much."

"Wow! That's really cool, Uncle Zak."

"Thanks," Uncle Zak beamed, then reached over and pressed the red button. Within seconds, the "pane" was gone. "See? The concentrated freezing has been stopped and the unfrozen water seeps back down into the thin basin at the base of the window frame. Easier than opening a stiff window."

"Everyone's going to want one of these!"

"I imagine so, but not right away. It's still rather an expensive prototype. So it might take some convincing before people would invest in it."

Paul pressed the green button again and watched the pane of ice reform itself, as seamless and transparent as any piece of glass. "Who wouldn't want one of these? I mean, so what if a baseball smashes your window? You press a button and the window fixes itself."

Uncle Zak's grin spread. "Yes. My original idea was to provide a safe and lasting window. But now I can see that there are other benefits. Just think, with these frames throughout your entire house, window washing will be a thing of the past. And I'm currently working on some of the water compounds to produce colored glass, mirrored glass, stained glass — all kinds of design effects."

"So what happens if you run out of water in the window frame?"

Uncle Zak walked over to his desk and grabbed a cylindrical plastic container with a peaked lid and went back to the window. "When you run out of water for the pane, you simply take a bottle of the water compound, insert it into this hole in the top of the frame, and squeeze. With a variety of compounds available, people can choose whatever type of 'glass' they want, and instantly have their special glass — no installation necessary."

Paul smiled. "It sounds like once this invention takes off, it will have endless possibilities. This is going to make you rich!"

Uncle Zak stopped, a frown creasing his forehead. "What's wrong, Uncle Zak?"

"I'm afraid to go out and patent this invention.

Every time I take one of my inventions out to be patented, someone else seems to have come up with the exact same idea. It's as if someone were watching me and stealing all of my ideas."

"I remember you mentioning that before, Uncle Zak. But last time you mentioned it, you said you thought someone was sneaking in here."

Uncle Zak stroked his chin. "Yes, I did. Then I noticed that my ideas don't get stolen until I take them out of the house."

"How do you usually take them to the patent office?" Paul asked.

"I've been renting a truck from the truck rental agency just down the street."

"Maybe we could be a little more sneaky this time."

"What do you mean?"

"Do you usually rent a small truck?" Paul asked.

"Yes," Uncle Zak said. "A cargo van."

"That has windows, doesn't it?"

Uncle Zak nodded.

"Then maybe this time we should rent a cube van or something big, without any way that people can see inside. And let's box the entire invention up in a large furniture or appliance box. Then it won't look like an invention. It will just look like we're moving some furniture."

Uncle Zak smiled and slapped Paul on the back. "My, my, you're becoming quite the analytical scientist, my boy."

"You've taught me well," Paul replied, blushing.

"Please excuse me for a few minutes. I'm going to go call the patent office to see if they can squeeze me in this afternoon. I also have to call the truck rental place. They almost always have a truck available on short notice." With that, Uncle Zak strode out of the lab, leaving Paul alone with the new invention.

He stood looking at the window for a minute, and then couldn't resist what came to mind.

Stepping forward, he first tapped the glass, then made a fist, and drove the fist through the glass. It shattered in a million pieces. Paul looked at his hand. No cuts. No blood. He grinned a huge grin and pressed the green button. The window frame hummed and the pane reformed itself.

"This is so cool."

Again, Paul put a hand through the window, this time using a left-handed karate chop. *Smash.* Again, no cuts, no blood.

He pressed the green button and the window hummed and reformed itself again.

"I've *got* to show this to some of my friends," Paul said, smiling. "It's going to crack them up when they think it's regular glass." He laughed.

This time, he chose a karate stance and then put his foot through the window.

Smash!

Green button. *Hum.* Reformed pane.

33

Mocking an announcer's voice, Paul giggled and said, "Please kids, don't try this at home." Then he leaned forward and put his forehead through the glass. His head shattered the pane easily, and once again there were no cuts, no glass, just the cool, clear water compound running down his face.

This time when he pressed the green button, it hummed, but nothing happened.

"Uh oh. Did I break it?" Paul looked around the room and spotted the small plastic bottles of water compound. "No. It's just out of water."

He walked over and picked up one of the plastic bottles and squeezed the contents into the hole in the top of the window frame. Then he pressed the green button.

The frame hummed and the pane reformed itself. This time, though, the window pane was completely black.

"Oh, no! Oh, no!" Something must've gone wrong, Paul thought. Maybe he'd injected the water compound in the wrong spot. He ran out of the lab to get his uncle.

"Uncle Zak!"

He met his uncle in the kitchen at the back of the house where he was speaking with someone on the phone. Uncle Zak gestured that he would be just

one minute. When he finished his phone call, he put the receiver down and turned to his nephew.
"What's wrong, Paul?"

"I think I did something to the window. I broke it, or something."

"What happened?" Uncle Zak asked and he headed back down the hallway with Paul following close behind.

"I was playing with it; breaking the glass and reforming the window," Paul said. "Then it ran out of water, so I injected more water compound into it. Only, this time it turned out black."

"Black?"

"Yes. You can't see anything through it!"

When they got back to the lab, they looked at the window. Only, the window wasn't black. It was clear. Transparent. Just like before.

Paul scratched his head. "Honest, Uncle Zak! It was black! I don't know what happened."

Uncle Zak picked up the plastic bottle sitting on the window ledge. "Is this the compound that you used?" he asked, sniffing it.

"Yes."

Uncle Zak laughed. "I think I know what happened."

"What?" Paul asked.

"This compound you injected is an extremely dense salt-water compound. Because there are more particles in salt water — namely, the salt particles — it takes light a little bit longer to pass through it. So when you first formed the pane, the light hadn't even passed all the way through the window. That's why the pane looked black. It likely took several minutes for the light to pass through."

"Freaky."

"It's similar to the stars we see at night. Most people know that some of the stars we see have likely burned out thousands of years ago, but that it takes the light so long to reach us, that, to us, they still appear to be there.

"I'd be very interested in testing the speed of the light through that window to see exactly how long it actually takes for it to pass through." Uncle Zak began stroking his chin and pacing back and forth. Suddenly, he stopped and turned toward the window.

A face appeared in the window — a wide, puffy face with black shadows under the eyes and a hideous-looking scowl.

"He's looking right at me!" Paul yelped.

"No, he's not," Uncle Zak said. "Remember, it takes the light several minutes to pass through the window. It's more likely that this ugly fellow was looking in the window a few minutes ago, before we were even back here. What he likely saw was an empty room."

"So he might not be standing there now?" Paul asked.

Uncle Zak suddenly grabbed his nephew by the arm. "C'mon, Paul! Let's hide! This guy could be the thief who's been stealing my invention ideas!"

They hurried toward the walk-in closet beside Uncle Zak's desk, keeping their eyes on the face in the window. The ugly man's eyes darted about the room, then he grinned before he sauntered away from the window.

"Quickly!" Uncle Zak said, ushering Paul into the closet.

Just as the closet door closed behind them, they heard footsteps entering the lab.

"We just made it," Uncle Zak said quietly, pulling his cell phone out of his back pocket. "Time to call the police."

Through a crack in the closet doorway, Paul watched the ugly man sneak around the room. He went to Uncle Zak's desk first, as if he'd been in the room before and knew exactly where everything was kept. He immediately spotted the cylindrical plastic containers with the water compound in them, grabbed one, and stuck the opening under one of his large nostrils. He squinted, as if trying to figure out the scent, then rifled through the desk drawers.

"The police are on their way," Uncle Zak whispered, edging closer to the closet door to have a peek. "Oh no! He's going to find my schematics for the window!"

As if on cue, a grin spread across the ugly man's face as he pulled out a manila envelope and peeked inside. He quickly folded the envelope and tucked it into his back pocket.

"He's going to get away with my invention idea," Uncle Zak whispered, "...unless I can stall him until the police arrive. You stay hidden in here, Paul."

Uncle Zak opened the closet door and stepped into the room.

"Hello," Uncle Zak said in a light, pleasant tone. "Can I help you?"

The ugly man looked shocked and his eyes darted back and forth as he attempted to stammer out a response.

"You must be with the moving company," Uncle Zak offered, handing the man an easy explanation.

"Y-yes, yes I am," the ugly man said, beginning to stand up straight. "There was no answer when I knocked, so I let myself in."

"That's great," Uncle Zak said. "Now, I was hoping that we could get started in this room. This desk and the book shelves need to be moved. Did you bring any boxes that I could store the books in?"

The ugly man walked over to the book shelves as if to examine them, and, hidden from Uncle Zak's view, he pulled out a knife.

Paul gasped loudly.

Startled, the ugly man looked toward the closet and spotted Paul through the crack. He stepped forward and yanked the closet door open. "Come out here!" he yelled, grabbing Paul by the arm and hauling him into the room. He shoved Paul in the direction of his uncle, keeping the knife pointed at them.

"Don't hurt the boy," Uncle Zak said, putting himself between his nephew and the knife-wielding man. "Take my invention; just don't hurt the boy."

"You stupid fool," the man said. "I've stolen every one of your inventions for the past year! I've been able to sell them for a good price, too."

"How have you done it?" Uncle Zak asked. "How did you know when to sneak in and steal the invention idea?"

"My brother owns the truck rental agency. Every time you phone to rent a truck, I know that you have another invention idea to sell. Then, it's a simple matter of waiting until you're not around, picking the lock, sneaking in, and grabbing the paperwork and plans."

The ugly man then noticed the cell phone in Uncle Zak's hand. "Wait a minute," he said. "Did you call the police?"

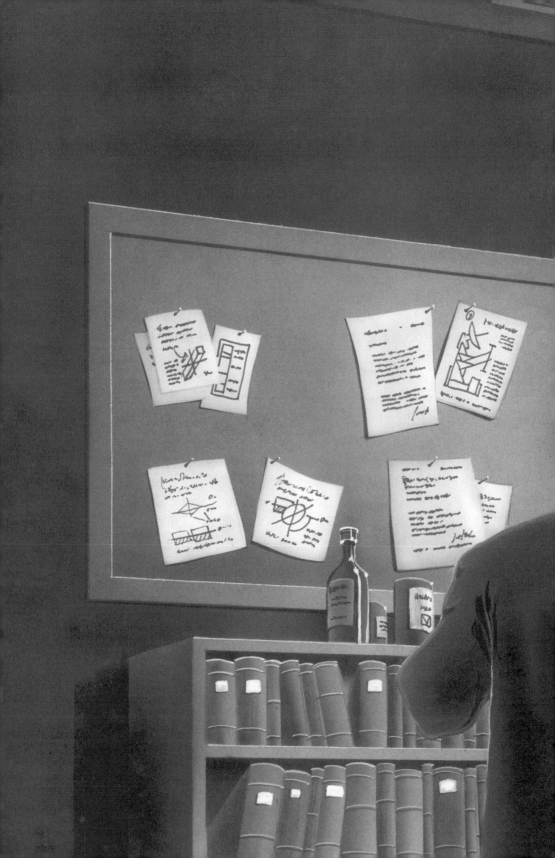

"I didn't have time," Uncle Zak said, shrugging.

The man scowled, then went to the window and peered outside. The street outside was quiet and empty, except for a young child on a bicycle speeding down the sidewalk. "Well, I'm going to keep one eye on the window, so I can see them coming."

Uncle Zak smirked and whispered to Paul out of the side of his mouth. "He isn't going to see anything out that window until it's too late."

"Now tell me," the ugly man said, waving the knife at Uncle Zak. "What other invention ideas do you have brewing that I can take with me today?"

Uncle Zak shrugged and looked around the room.

"You must have something. Even some unfinished notes. Those would still be worth a little bit of money."

Just then a police car raced down the street and pulled into the driveway.

"Rats! The cops are here!" The man began to run out of the den, on his way to the back door. But just as he got to the den door, a police officer pounced on him, wrestled the knife out of his hand, and slapped a handcuff on his wrist. Another officer covered the man with his gun.

As the thief was being cuffed and dragged away, the man stared blankly at the officers. "How did you get out of your car and into the house so fast? It should have taken you at least a few minutes! I don't understand! I had time to get away!"

Uncle Zak laughed and jabbed his nephew with his elbow as the police dragged their quarry away. "C'mon, Paul. Let's head outside so we can look in through the window and watch the police tackle that crook again."

The Doom of Planet D

by Alison Baird

When the inhabitants of the fourth planet from the star 11041536-G finally fled their home in despair, thundering through the skies in immense silver starships, they left behind them cities already crumbling in decay. It would not take long for those once-majestic structures to become ruins, half covered in vegetation or buried in creeping sands.

The people took care, however, to leave behind one high-powered radio beacon. Its message, designed to repeat endlessly for centuries to come, would caution any approaching ship to stay away from the abandoned world with its deadly contagion. *DANGER! DANGER!* the beacon warned, piercing the planet's tainted atmosphere to pass far out into the void of interstellar space.

Unfortunately, the scout ship from Earth which arrived a thousand years later did not quite understand the message.

"At last!" the ship's captain exclaimed in delight and excitement to her crew as the coded message came through the com. "After all these centuries, someone is finally sending us an invitation!"

● ❧

The new world was dubbed Planet D, and the survey ship *Magellan* was quickly dispatched to study it. The research teams eagerly pored over the new planet's patchwork of barren wastelands and rambling swamps. The scout ship's mechanized probes had revealed an atmosphere much like the Earth's, free of any harmful microbes, so the explorers could go about their work quickly and efficiently without any need for cumbersome helmets or environment suits. The most exciting find had

50

been the ruins, still visible from space as faint grid patterns half hidden in vegetation or sand. Once the biologists got over their disappointment at not finding any live intelligent beings, they left the ruins for the archaeological teams to peruse and began searching for other life-forms. But when the ruins were freed from their sandy tombs and leafy coverings, the biologists' excitement was revived.

Experts, studying the crumbling concrete-like substance of which the structures were made, pronounced them to be the work of a species with strong similarities to humans. There had been buildings, bridges, and paved roads on this planet. And when remains of the aliens were at last uncovered, they did indeed prove to be bipedal vertebrates with a definite upright posture.

"Humans — or something very like us!" the chief biologist declared. "Well, why not? After all, there have been cases of parallel evolution on Earth: sharks and dolphins look somewhat similar, even though they're not closely related. Why shouldn't there be parallel developments of life-forms on different worlds?"

There were also a few animal remains uncovered, but not many: surprisingly few, in fact, for a planet this size. And for a long time, no living things were observed apart from the trees and plants: and even these seemed sickly. This ecosystem was clearly not healthy. No large groups of herd animals were seen straggling across the barrens. No large creatures wallowed in the water of the swamps or swam in the large seas.

When at last some living organisms were discovered, the researchers could not believe what they saw.

•

"I don't believe it!" Bill Rogers exclaimed.

The senior archaeologist stood in the center of a clearing surrounded by vine-tangled ruins. The large oblong space before him was full of animals: furred, mammalian creatures for the most part, though a few birds were fluttering about the vegetation-covered tops of broken walls. All were completely tame, as is often the case in areas where humans have never been before: the animals simply did not know to be afraid. A few came right up to the research team members, rubbing against their ankles, jumping onto their shoulders, purring and crooning and grunting affectionately. As Rogers stood there, a thing like a pink feather boa approached him, progressing inchworm-fashion across the cracked pavement. It coiled about his ankle, peering up at him with two bright button eyes. "Burble!" it said winningly.

"It's like a kids' petting zoo," Rogers said, shaking his head.

Sally Janes, the chief biologist, nodded her neat red head. "All the life-forms here are like this," she said.

He stared at the creatures. There were rodents resembling large guinea pigs; animated teddy bears stumping around on their hind legs; fluffy, flightless birds like walking featherdusters. "They all look quite different to me."

"But have you noticed there aren't many large ones? There's nothing the size of a deer or a bear. Most are slightly to very much smaller than a human child. That's why the aerial probes didn't see any of them: they're all so tiny. And they're all furred or feathered animals too: the equivalents of our mammals and birds back on Earth. There's nothing here that resembles a reptile or an amphibian."

"So?" asked the young botanist who was busy examining the vines covering a nearby wall.

"It makes no sense, Joe," Sally told him. "In any ecosystem you have diversification of species. Warm-blooded and cold-blooded animals, plant eaters, meat eaters, water and land dwellers, climbers and burrowers. All in a wide variety of sizes and shapes..."

"But that's on Earth," Joe pointed out. "This is an alien planet."

"It just seems...odd. And there's another peculiarity. Have you noticed their eyes?"

Rogers glanced down at the pink creature, which was climbing his leg like a giant caterpillar, then looked at the other little creatures playing about the ruins. Fluffy yellow birds like Easter chicks... oversized hamsters... roly-poly teddy bears. There were some tiny, hoofed creatures, like deer shrunk to the size of rabbits, which he would have taken for infants had they not been accompanied by even tinier offspring. The creatures were really as different as could be except for their small size.

And their eyes.

Everywhere he looked, huge melting orbs of blue or amber or chocolate-brown looked up at him appealingly. Sally stooped to pick up a squirrel-tailed animal, small enough to fit in her pocket, and held it out to him. "This one reminds me of a tiny African primate called a bush baby. Bush babies have huge eyes like these because they're nocturnal animals. Any animal that feeds by night needs very large eyes to collect whatever light is available. Look at owls, for instance, or cats." She put the creature down again and it scampered off to join its fellows. "But these animals are all diurnal, perfectly at ease in daylight. It just doesn't make sense."

A pale-blue bird with the bulging eyes of a nightjar flew overhead, singing sweetly. Rogers looked at it with distaste. Unwinding the fuzzy pink boa from his shoulders, he placed it on the ground.

"Cartoons," he said, in a tone of annoyance.

"What?" The other two stared at him.

The older man looked disgusted. "Didn't you kids ever study history? Cartoons were animated drawings, done by hand back in the twentieth century. One man founded a huge entertainment empire based on his cartoons."

"So what about them?" asked Joe impatiently.

"These animals remind me of cartoons. In old-style animation, you see, people and animals weren't usually portrayed realistically. They tended to have exaggerated features: big, round heads as large as their bodies, outsized eyes." He gestured at the frolicking wildlife. "This bunch are more like living cartoons than anything real."

"Are you saying they've been genetically modified?" said Joe doubtfully. "I don't think these people ever got to that level of technology."

"No, that's true," Rogers admitted. "This race had a fairly low-tech culture: a few land and air vehicles, hydroelectric dams, nuclear reactors, that sort of thing. But their civilization was mainly based on agriculture and nonrenewable resources. However, their space program seems to have been a rapid development."

"Yes — as if they had a sudden pressing need to escape from their own planet," remarked Joe.

Sally nodded. "Well, naturally! They ruined the place. Look at all those deserts and wastelands: the studies show they were all forested once. The surviving forests are dying. And the seas are empty except for a few crustaceans and primitive squid-like mollusks. Where are the fish? They must have existed: there's a missing vertebrate link. The only explanation is that they were overharvested. No, these people had no advanced scientific capabilities like biological engineering, or they'd have at least tried to fix the damage they did."

"I agree. But it still goes against the grain to think that Mother Nature could have produced anything as cloyingly cute as those critters," said Rogers.

"There are some cute animals on Earth," said Joe.

"Some. But have you come across *anything* here that isn't a wee, cuddly, cute beastie with goo-goo eyes?" Joe and Sally shook their heads. "What are the odds against that? Where's the biodiversity?"

"Some evolutionary advantage must have been involved," said Sally frowning. "Every species adapts to its environment, or it can't survive. So ..." Her eyes widened in sudden horror, and she seized Rogers' arm. "Oh no. We've got to get off this planet!"

"What? Why?" Joe asked.

"I just realized why these people had to flee — what destroyed their world! Captain!" She called urgently into her com. "Tell everyone to get back on board ship! There's a deadly biohazard on this planet!"

"Has anyone been contaminated?" came the captain's voice over the com.

Sally was already running. "I hope not," she panted into the instrument, "but it's a possibility. We've all got to get out of here now!"

●●

Later, as the *Magellan* blasted back into the safety of space, the researchers and crew members pressed Sally hard for an explanation.

"Those beings down on that planet were like us, all right," she said grimly. "*How* like us they were! Back in our twentieth and twenty-first centuries, we were doing all the same things: clear-cutting and strip-mining, overpopulating the Earth. And the animals were getting squeezed out. Many species couldn't survive the destruction of their habitat."

"But lots of people were active in saving the environment too," Joe commented. "The public wanted to rescue species from extinction."

"Oh, sure," said Sally bitterly. "*Some* species. Everyone was worried about saving the panda and the koala bear, the dolphins and the baby seals. But what about the tiger, the crocodile, and the great white shark? No one cared about them: they

59

were big and fierce, ugly or menacing-looking, and they'd been known to kill human beings. Still, they played vital roles in their ecosystems, controlling the population growth of other species, maintaining the balance of the food chain. But little woolly seal pups and chubby pandas are cute, tigers and crocs weren't. So they were allowed to die out. The white rhino wasn't cute enough: it, too, became extinct. And the bats that lived in the rainforests, helping pollinate the trees and spread their seeds: they were absolutely indispensable to that ecosystem, but biologists couldn't stop people from killing them, or get the rest of the world interested in saving them. Bats weren't cute, they were associated with witches and haunted houses and getting tangled in people's hair, nonsense like that. So, bye-bye bats."

A silence fell. Then Rogers spoke up. "You're saying that the animal species on Planet D adapted somehow?"

She nodded. "There are precedents. Industrial melanism is one. Back when the industrial revolution caused whole areas of Britain to become tainted with soot, a variety of moth developed with a dark coloring to provide camouflage on blackened walls and tree trunks. What happened was that the light-colored moths of that species were all eaten by predators, since they couldn't disguise themselves any more. The few darker moths survived, and soon the whole species had the sooty coloring. The species adapted to new environmental conditions *in less than a century*!

"What we've seen on Planet D is the same phenomenon," she continued. "The survival of the fittest or in this case, the cutest. These animals have been *cutified*. It's a proven fact that humans are drawn not only to our own infants, but to anything small and big-eyed and helpless: kittens, puppies, baby seals. Even machines: a small hovercar, say, designed with extra-large headlights is endearing to us. Oh look, we say, isn't that *cute*! Our natural protective instinct has been activated. So on Planet D, only those organisms that most resembled infants, the tiny, appealing, helpless-looking ones, were saved by the humanoids from extinction while all the other life-forms were permitted to die out. The cute ones went on to have generations of offspring, each more adorable and irresistible than the last. No humanoid could bear to kill any of them: it would be like murdering a baby! The result was that the Planet D species, who were manipulated unintentionally by the humanoids, ended up manipulating them in turn. They must have spread all over the planet, unchecked by the humanoids or by any predator (all those nasty meat eaters, of course, were long gone), helping to ruin the already burdened biosphere, and finally forcing the people to flee."

"I still don't see why you call this a biohazard," said Joe rather sulkily. "Where's the danger in..."

"Joe," interrupted Rogers, "why is your backpack burbling?"

The crew members all turned to stare at the botanist's equipment pack, which was stirring and emitting strange noises. Sheepishly, Joe opened the pack and drew out a pink feather boa. One end lifted, cooed softly, and gazed at the onlookers with wide, blue eyes.

The captain frowned. "Joe, you know the penalties for smuggling alien species to Earth!"

"It's only a *little* one," he said blushing. "And I have a kid at home who'd love it."

"And then all the other children will see your kid's pet," added Sally, "and they'll all want one, and the next thing you know everyone will be coming to Planet D to catch animals and sell them on Earth. And some will inevitably get loose, and reproduce themselves, and disrupt the balance of *our* ecosystems. They'll overrun our planet the way they did their own."

"Joe, throw that thing out the airlock!" ordered the captain.

At once there were howls of anguish and several crew members sprang up automatically to surround the animal. Sally laughed without humor. "You see?" she told them. "You can't do it: your own protective parental instincts won't allow you to harm this little creature."

The captain sighed. "Take us back to the planet," she commanded the pilots, "and set us down on the surface just long enough for Joe here to free that little pink menace. And put in a message to Earth headquarters. Planet D contains a contagious biohazard. No one, repeat, *no one* is to make any unauthorized landings there!"

Sally shook her head and heaved a sigh. Would their warning be enough? she wondered.

In Joe's arms, the boa burbled.

Catching Rays

by James Van Pelt

Wendy stood on tiptoe on the edge of the chair to adjust another mirror in the corner of her room, squinting her sea-green eyes to aim it. "Lots of scientific discoveries happen by accident."

Her best friend, Rupert, lay on the bed reading *Sky and Telescope*. There were articles on the Mars colony and Earth-like planets the new star probes had discovered. A little box filled with computer disks sat next to him. "Uh huh," he said. He turned another page. "So are you setting up a discovery or an accident?"

Wendy looked at him keenly, but he didn't appear to be laughing. She said, "This experiment may get me a spot on the colony ship. Besides, not everything we learn is on purpose. Look at Newton."

The next mirror hung above Wendy's favorite star colony recruitment poster. A family, their faces glowing with hope, stood on a hill overlooking a valley filled with alien trees and weird animals. The sign underneath read, "Only the best will go."

Rupert rolled over and held the magazine above him. He said, "An apple hit Newton on the head."

"There you go, and that started his theories about gravity. Doctors weren't looking for penicillin when they found it. Some mold grew on a petri dish. Same with X rays and the quantum space drive. So a scientist has to keep her eyes open, otherwise she'll miss the happy accidents."

"What are you trying to prove here? Is this another one of your light projects? I don't get this fascination with light." He eyed the mirrors scattered throughout the room. Wendy had stuck them on the walls, ceiling, and furniture.

She concentrated on the last mirror. The tape didn't hold well, and it slipped. She said, "I'm going to demonstrate that light loses intensity when it's reflected. And, yes, this is one of my light projects. You love astronomy... I don't see that investigating light is any different."

Rupert put the magazine down. "The first colony starships are going to need astronomers. I figure I have a better chance of going if I get a head start now. There aren't going to be any sixth graders next year in the whole world who know more than I do about the galaxy, I can tell you that. So studying the stars makes sense. They'll have to choose me. You're just puttering around here." He looked at the now completed mirror arrangement. "Although it's pretty cool puttering."

Wendy said, "Experimental science is the basis for new knowledge. Who knows what they'll find on the new worlds? They'll need 'putterers' like me. I think they'll take kids on the trip based on their scientific *potential*. Not on whether they've memorized a lot of star names." She grinned at him. "Now, are you going to help? I'm about ready." Wendy crossed to her desk where she had set up a laser pointer on a work stand.

"As long as I get to use your mom's computer afterwards. I've got the latest pictures from my telescope, and I need to see how they turned out. So what's your plan?" Rupert asked.

Wendy checked the laser's alignment. "I'm going to turn on the laser. The light will go from here to the first mirror..." She pointed to a corner where a mirror hung over a poster of a rainbow. "...where it will be reflected to that mirror." She shifted her finger to a second mirror on her headboard. "To that mirror, to that one, to that one, to that one, to that one, and so on until it ends up here, on this piece of paper." She pointed to a bull's-eye drawn on a notepad on her desk. "Along the way, I'll measure how much weaker the light grows with each reflection."

"How will you do that?" Rupert scratched his chin.

"Visually. That's where you come in. When I tell you to, turn on the fan on my dresser. It will blow across that tray full of flour. Then I'll be able see the laser's path."

Rupert shook his head doubtfully. "OK. It'll be like a light show, right?"

"Well, this is just a crude demonstration. By the time the science fair comes around, I'll have something more impressive."

Rupert smiled. "Like last year when your display melted?"

"Are you going to keep bringing that up?" Wendy said as she flicked the laser on, and a bright, red spot appeared in the bull's-eye. She paused dramatically. "Turn on the fan."

Rupert flipped the switch. The fan kicked into life much harder than Wendy had expected. She'd imagined a faint, white cloud, cut by glittering strings of ruby laser light. Instead, flour exploded from the tray in a choking fog.

"Argh! Turn it off!" Wendy squeezed her eyes shut, but it was too late. The first spray caught her full in the face.

"I...can't...find it," said Rupert. Wendy couldn't tell if he was laughing or coughing. She staggered toward the fan's sound, banging her shin against a stool she didn't remember putting in the middle of the room. Rupert stumbled into her. He was definitely laughing.

He said, "Hooooo. Hoooo! I'm a fog horn. Watch out for the reef!"

After she turned the fan off, it took some time for the flour to settle. They retreated to the hall. When she saw Rupert, she started giggling. Flour coated him from head to toe. His eyes blinked out at her like two dark marbles on a snow field. He shook his head, flinging white powder everywhere.

"What will you tell your mom?" said Rupert.

Wendy looked at the base of her closed bedroom door, where a haze of flour had drifted out. "I'll say it was a *scientific* accident. You should see your clothes! How will you explain this when you get home?"

Rupert said, "I'll tell them I was here. They'll understand. Now can we look at my pictures?" He held up his box of computer disks, also covered with flour.

After going outside to brush off most of the flour, they went into the office to use the computer. Rupert had been working on his science fair project for six months, a wall map of the night sky. He'd taken pictures with a digital camera through his telescope, then used the computer to print the images after he labeled the stars. Wendy's mom had the best printer in the neighborhood.

Rupert said, "I took new pictures of the stars north of the Little Dipper. I thought last week's were hazy. We need to compare."

Wendy wiped flour from each disk carefully until she found the two latest ones. She put the first disk in the computer and a scattering of stars appeared on the screen. "Is this the right one?" She didn't know the night sky as well as Rupert, and, to her, one set of stars looked pretty much the same as any other.

Rupert concentrated on the image. "Yes. Those brighter stars there and there are part of the con-stellation, Cassiopeia, on the northern horizon. See, if you connect them they look like the letter 'W.' That's the direction the first star probes went, the ones that didn't report back. The successful ones went toward Scorpius on the southern horizon."

"You're showing off," said Wendy, as she adjusted the image to make it clearer.

He didn't say anything, so she knew she was right. "OK, now I'll switch to this week's picture."

A new picture flicked on the screen. "Looks the same," she said.

"Here, let me see," said Rupert. He took the chair and hit the button that changed from one image to the next. "No, this one definitely isn't as good." The old picture and the new picture swapped places several times. Wendy still could see no difference. Rupert flipped them back and forth quickly.

Wendy sat up suddenly. "Do that again!"

"What?" Rupert rested his fingers on the keys.

"Switch them fast." She leaned closer to the computer monitor.

The pictures flicked one to the other.

"Stars aren't supposed to move, are they?" she said.

"What?" Rupert stared at her.

"That star changes position from this picture to the next. Look!" She put her finger on a crisp spot on the screen, then hit the key that switched to the other picture. The spot had moved about a centimeter.

"Wow!" said Rupert. "Let's see what star that is." He changed to the astronomy program on the computer and looked up that section of the sky. "Double wow! There isn't supposed to be a star there at all. I've found something!"

"I found it," said Wendy.

Rupert went on, his face glowing with excitement. "They'll name it after me. I'll be famous! I'll bet it's a comet. Rupert's Comet. I like the sound of that. They'll have to take me on the starship if I found a comet. No other sixth grader has ever done that, I'll bet."

Wendy said, "I spotted it first."

He grabbed her hand and shook it. "Oh, of course you did. It'll be the Rupert-Wendy Comet. We'll both be famous!" Rupert jumped around the room, shedding floury puffs.

Wendy stayed in front of the computer, thinking. "Are you sure it's a comet? We need to be scientific about this."

"What do you mean? Naturally, it's a comet. What else could it be?" Rupert sat in his chair, raising another small cloud.

"We don't want to tell everyone we found a comet when that might not be what it is. We'd look like silly kids. For example, do you know if it's coming toward us or going away?"

Rupert leaned back, still excited. He drummed his fingers on the desk. "It's new, so it must be coming toward us."

Wendy nodded. "That's good thinking. Let's test it another way, though. Here's last week's image." She pointed to the screen. "Now, I'll darken it until the new object disappears." A tiny control bar appeared on the screen, and she used it to dim the image until they couldn't see the new spot. The control button was turned halfway down. "We'll do the same with the fresh picture." This time the new spot didn't disappear until the control button was three-quarters turned down. "See, the star is brighter, so that means you're right. It's coming closer. How else can we test that it's a comet? What's a comet look like through a telescope?"

Rupert closed his eyes as if he were reading from an astronomy book in his head. "A comet is a ball of icy rock. When it gets close to the sun, the ice starts to boil off and makes the trail behind it. Since my telescope is pretty small, this comet should be close. It would be fuzzy in the picture because the sun would be melting it."

"Uh huh," said Wendy. She increased the magnification so they saw less of the sky and could concentrate on their mystery spot. It shone on the screen like a tiny diamond, clear and bright and not fuzzy at all.

Wendy looked at the image for a while, running possibilities through her head. Finally she said, "It's darned bright. Look, it's brighter than half the stars on the screen. If it's not a comet, then it's either very shiny, like a mirror, or very big, or very close. Is your telescope set up?"

Rupert nodded.

"OK. I'll grab some equipment from my lab..."

"Your 'lab' is your bedroom," said Rupert.

"When I'm doing an experiment, it's my lab. And that's not the point anyway. I'll meet you in your backyard. Better brush the rest of that flour off before you go into your house or your dad will kill me. No! No! Not in here! Wait until you're outside."

When Wendy reached Rupert's backyard, he'd already aimed the telescope toward the northern horizon. Stars glittered like fiery sand scattered on black cloth. There was no moon or clouds. Perfect conditions for star gazing.

"What's that?" asked Rupert doubtfully.

On the grass, Wendy unpacked a small box containing a battery pack and a complicated-looking device. "This is a spectrometer. It's a machine that can tell you what something is made of by the light it makes when it burns. Like a lit candle will produce a different kind of light than if you burn a piece of paper. The spectrometer can measure the difference. Scientists use much better ones than this to decide what kind of chemicals are in stuff. They'll burn a sample and the spectrometer will look at the flame. See, I told you my 'puttering around' with light would be useful. I just didn't know it would be this soon." She attached the spectrometer to the telescope.

"What kind of kid owns a spectrometer?" said Rupert.

Wendy grinned in the dark. "One who doesn't spend her allowance on stuff like music videos and junk food, and who's going to be on the first colony starship, that's who."

"So, what do you think you can find out by looking at the light?" Rupert held the telescope steady while she checked the spectrometer.

"Let's be scientific about it. How come we can see the mystery spot?" asked Wendy.

"Same reason we see the moon and planets," said Rupert promptly. "It reflects the sun's light."

"That's one way," she said as she switched on the spectrometer. A tiny screen glowed on its top. "If the mystery spot is *reflecting* the sun, I'll know because the reflected light will be similar to sunlight. You can tell some things about the sun by looking at the light that bounces off the moon. Are you sure we're pointed at our target?"

Rupert checked the telescope's aim through a smaller telescope mounted on its barrel. "Yes, right on it."

Wendy stayed hunched over the spectrometer for a long time. A summer breeze moved through the trees behind them. She looked at the numbers on the small screen, growing more and more excited. Her cheeks warmed as she realized what she had suspected was true. "It's not reflecting the sun. It's making its own light," she said.

"What is it then?" Rupert's voice sounded small in the outdoors. He sounded a little frightened.

"I think it's a spaceship, Rupert. A really big one. I think we're looking at a space ship slowing down as it's coming toward us, and its engines are on."

Rupert glanced up at the sky, to the tiny star in Cassiopeia that wasn't supposed to be there. "We don't have any space ships in that direction. That's where we sent the probes that didn't come back."

Wendy sat on the grass and gazed at the new star. "Exactly. I think our probes reached somebody, though. I think some aliens are coming for a visit!"

W endy and Rupert's discovery caused a lot of excitement. Thousands of scientists pointed their telescopes toward Cassiopeia. They sent messages to the travelers coming to Earth and found out that they were as curious about us as we were about them.

In the excitement, the two friends almost forgot about the colony starships, and if they would be able to go, until they both received letters saying that other children had been chosen.

Their disappointment didn't last long, though. On the same day, a man came to Wendy's house to talk with Wendy and Rupert and their parents. He was a small man with lots of gray hair, but he laughed a lot and soon made everyone feel relaxed.

He introduced himself as the chief coordinator of a new space mission. "The alien ship is designed to travel between the stars, not land on planets, so we've decided to send our best people into space to welcome our new, alien friends. They said they would like to know all of us: scientists, artists, teachers, and traders. They also want to meet our children. The committee has chosen you two to go as our representatives."

Wendy and Rupert looked at each other, but they didn't speak.

The man said, "Will you go? We think that you have earned the right because you made the important discovery."

Wendy grinned and said, "Oh, it was just an accident."

Rupert smiled too and said, "A *scientific* accident."

Wendy laughed. She was so excited that she could hardly sit still. *They were going!* "All we did was keep our eyes open."

Shine

by Beverley J. Meincke

Sleek and white, the arrow sliced across the browser screen, back and forth, obeying every command of Danny's hand on the mouse. He allowed it to linger over a block of text, something about how great this nature magazine was. As if he cared. Danny watched his arrow morph into a capital I, a brave soldier of the realm, that with a single click could snatch up all those boring words and blast them to Jupiter. Well, maybe not. Danny led his arrow toward the row of blah gray icons across the top of the screen. One-by-one, he zapped them with its magic color gun. The stop sign — *bang!* — red. The house, the sundial thingie…

Boring, boring, bor-ing.

"Look," Danny remembered his mother saying, "when the cursor becomes a little hand — see there? — it points your way to the whole world." A cool breeze through his open bedroom window pointed the way to the driveway. And his basketball hoop. Winking at him in the moonlight, it seemed to say, "Forget about that silly science project. Come and play!"

It was too dark. Besides, Mom would ground him for a year.

No. He'd better let that ridiculous, cartoon owl riding a spaceship across this web page help him choose an insect to research. He stared at it. It stared back. Then, just to bug him, it winked. Danny felt like punching its lights out. And those stars splattered all over the page — oh, brother! They made it look like the bathroom mirror after Danny flossed his teeth. He leaned in closer to the screen, so close that even though the picture was mostly black the light hurt his eyes. Hey! Maybe if he went blind, Mom and Mrs. Pritchard would let him off the hook.

The screen crackled and snatched at his hair. *Cool!* He snatched it back with a swipe of his finger. His breath condensed on the glass when he laughed in two big smudges. Hey, even cooler! *Snort!* Take that, dumb owl!

This close, Danny could see that the pictures were made up of square specks of colored light, each one squished in between its neighbors, kind of like super figures on display at the toy store. Danny looked away from the harsh light and closed his eyes. Big chunky letters in the page's banner wouldn't go away. He watched them sparkle and dance on the backs of his eyelids. How come they weren't red anymore, Danny wondered, but suddenly kind of bluish?

The image of the letters faded, but Danny's imagination didn't. He began to see their specks of light as little bug-eyed creatures hanging out on their graph-paper grid.

Newton yawned and stretched. Well, he tried to stretch; there wasn't enough room.

"Ouch!"

Newton glared at his grid-neighbor to the right.

"You shove me, I shove you back. It's only fair."

"Sorry, Wick," Newton said, even though he wasn't. Being jolted awake by the Great Designer, when Mother Cathode's cycles began, always left Newton a little grumpy. He liked being switched off. In his dreams he could be whatever color he wanted to be. "Just because you get to show yourself off as chartreuse today."

"Green with envy are we, Mr. Fifty-percent-gray?"

"Oh, stop it. I was only trying to..."

"Please! Not another day of your whining about how crowded it is on the grid."

"Wick, you are such a square. Don't you ever wonder what a good stretch would feel like?"

"Square am I? *Well!* Look around, buddy. We're *all* square. We're pixels, picture elements on a computer screen. We're *supposed* to be square."

"What if I don't want to be?"

"Brother! Next you'll be raving about leaving the grid."

Newton brightened at the thought.

"You're joking."

He wasn't. Newton often dreamed about visiting the pixels on that other monitor screen, the one that had faced them ever since out-of-the-box. Curious... sometimes it radiated pictures that jumped right out at you, colors bright enough to be real. Sometimes it rested in darkness, like now. "You know what I think, Wick?"

Wick laughed so hard he could barely speak. "Think?" More laughter. "You know you — no — *everybody* would be a lot happier if you'd just follow Father Pantone's instructions, and quit *thinking*."

"Father Pantone..." Newton scoffed. "Ever-meddling Color Governor and Matchmaker...the

almighty scheme of things...I know." He sighed. "But what about *me*?"

"Me, me, me... Since you're so full of questions, here's one: Why does it always have to be about *you*?"

Newton gasped just as Mother Cathode cycled. "Wick!" he sputtered, coughing up a mouthful of electrons.

Wick moaned. "Now what?"

"There! There it goes again!" Newton's phosphors sizzled with excitement.

"Yeah — your full-of-beams imagination."

Newton wriggled madly. "No. There... On the... Over there!"

"Where?"

"Are you switched off?" Dancing across the gigantic screen across the way was a solitary pixel, brighter than any Newton had ever seen. He was mesmerized. "How does he do that? *I* want to do that."

"Proper pixels wouldn't think of it."

"You dullard, you're afraid!" Newton couldn't stop trembling. "Imagine — to be *free*, instead of forever squashed into one spot." He watched the pixel flash six times quickly, swoop across the dark screen, and — "Where did he go?" A moment later it rose up in a long glowing trail of saffron-yellow light, then flashed six times again. Newton could hardly contain himself.

"Will you sit still!"

"I'm trying."

"Try harder!"

This gave Newton an idea. He curled up tight, sucking in cycle after cycle until he couldn't hold another electron. Ready to burst from all that energy, he gritted his teeth, focused, and pushed, glowing for all he was worth.

It was no use. Outshone by the likes of Wick and the others, plain old fifty-percent-gray would never attract the attention of someone as exquisite as the pixel across the way.

But wait! Maybe...

It came to rest on its tremendous screen. Newton closed his eyes, imagining he could feel its radiance on his face. Excitement began building in him again until he thought he'd bust a phosphor. Static crackled around him, his ears popped, then...

Snap!

A tingle ran down Newton's spine. He stretched out a hand. No one complained. A foot. Nothing! A wave of something he'd never felt before swept through him, making him feel as if he'd lose his electrons. Warmth surrounded him. Not from Mother Cathode's offerings — they were nowhere to be felt. He opened his eyes, just a crack, in time to see the Great Designer's plump fingertip pulling away from his grid. Nothing odd about that, the Great Designer often reached out and tapped this screen as if to say, "Well done." His fingertip should be moving away by now. Newton glanced up, and nearly fainted. *It* wasn't. His *grid* was!

He was riding the Great Designer's fingertip.

He was free!

"Help!" he heard someone squeal, then realized it was himself. All he could do was cling to his fleshy perch and...

Scream!

"Hey, Mom!" Newton heard the Great Designer call.

"What is it, Danny?"

"Come here...quickly, or you'll miss it."

"Look," Newton heard the Great Designer say. He couldn't.

Thud!

Where was he now? Newton blinked and looked around. Could it be? Yes! The screen across the way! The Great Designer's finger was touching it. Newton leapt off and onto its grid. Strange... this grid was divided into squares as it should be, but they were enormous, cold and metallic, shimmering silver in the light of his own screen, now the one across the way. And all empty — not a single pixel anywhere. A gentle hum reminded Newton of Mother Cathode. And of how hungry he was. He waited for a cycle. It never came. Instead, the hum grew louder and soon the whole grid began to quake. Newton held on as the giant pixel he'd seen earlier swooped past him and landed not far away.

It was even more magnificent close-up. And bigger! Newton opened his mouth. Nothing came out. He cleared his throat. "H-hello."

"Who goes there?"

The words rang so loudly that Newton not only heard them, but felt them in his belly as well. "I-I do."

"Show yourself."

"Down here. Do you suppose you could speak a little quieter?"

The pixel turned until it seemed to switch off. Then, out of the darkness a creature took shape, terrible and looming, its long, thin legs carrying a massive black body toward him. When it stopped, gigantic wings folded in across its back and disappeared. It lowered its painted head, revealing a wiry pair of antenna swiping at the air. Newton was very proud of himself for not screaming when he found himself scooped up by one of them and brought face-to-face with an enormous pair of eyes, perfectly round and of an orange he'd never been before. A wave of saffron light washed over Newton from the creature's underbelly. He gasped. "This is no monitor! This grid I'm on is the screen in a *real* window. And you're not a pixel."

"I don't recall suggesting I was. A what?"

"Pixel," Newton said proudly. "What I am." He demonstrated by turning himself pure white.

The creature flicked its antenna, very nearly

tossing Newton off. "What manner of magic is this? Fireflies are the only ones capable of such things."

"Then, you're a firefly?"

"Indeed. Lieutenant Versicolor Joule of Her Majesty's Royal Guard, at your service. Now if you'll excuse me, I'm on a quest."

"I love quests! What's a quest?"

Chuckling to himself, Joule bent his head and placed Newton gently onto the windowsill, spread his magnificent wings, and lifted off.

"You can't just leave me here!"

Joule stopped, hovering. "Little speck, there is no place for you in my quest to rid the kingdom of Queen Lampyridia, the Trickster."

"I'm confused. Didn't you just say you *worked* for the queen?"

"Lampyridia is not *my* queen."

"But she's a firefly."

"You mustn't hold that against us all."

"And a trickster?"

"Yes, plotting to destroy her sister's people."

"You."

Joule nodded.

Newton flinched. "How does she feel about pixels?"

"I don't imagine she's ever met one."

"Then maybe I can help. I can be pretty tricky myself. Watch." Newton became blue and aimed himself at Joule's underbelly, turning it pure white."

"My lantern!" Joule howled. "What have you done?"

"Relax!" Newton switched himself to green, giving Joule's underbelly a slightly bluish tint. "Better?"

"I wish to be as I was."

"Oh, brother, I'm still surrounded by squares!" Newton became yellow. "Happy?"

"Indeed. Now, tell me how this is done."

"Take me on your quest and I'll tell you along the way."

"Tricky indeed, little speck." Joule landed and offered Newton an antenna.

"My name's not Speck, it's Newton." He climbed up and they flew off.

Newton and Joule enjoyed getting to know each other. Newton told Joule all about grid life, how pixels — according to RGB law — made pictures with light. He forgave Joule for not knowing that that meant mixing red, green, and blue, because, after all, he was only a firefly. Joule taught Newton his pattern of light signals which, to demonstrate RGB, they practised together in more colors than even Father Pantone could have ordered.

"One more time, little speck. Magenta again, I quite enjoyed the feeling of reddish-blue."

"Newton — remember? And my phosphors ache."

"Right then, tiny friend, crawl onto my back. There, you won't need to hold on so tightly. I'd best get back to my quest, anyway. I'm afraid our game has quite made me forget my duties."

The two flew on in silence for a time. Newton was happy to rest. "Tell me about Queen Lampyridia," he said finally.

"She flies about our kingdom imitating our light patterns."

"Why?"

"In hopes of being mistaken for one of us."

"Then what?"

"We approach, only to discover too late that she is not."

"And then?"

"It's too dreadful to speak of."

"Where does she come from?" Newton continued to watch the ground go by while he listened to Joule's answer, interrupting when he thought he saw something. "Down there — a flash. Is it her?"

Joule slowed to a hover. He flashed his lantern six times quickly. "Hold on," he warned his passenger, then swooped into a lighted dive. Something fluttered past them, over them, and when Joule turned to complete his pattern, it had caught them in its flowing, white grid. Newton couldn't look. He buried his eyes while they were jostled about, shoved out of whatever they were caught in and into something else, something hard that gave a high-pitched ring when Joule's silky wings beat against it. "It's *her*, isn't it?"

"No, my tiny friend. A child has caught us."

"A child?"

"A small human who hunts with a net — imitating our call with a flashlight."

"We're all going to die!" This wail was from an unfamiliar voice. Newton peered out from behind Joule's head. Light of a thousand phosphors bit into his eyes, brilliant and yellow, coming from every-where. As his eyes adjusted, Newton saw that there were half-a-grid's-worth of fireflies trapped along with them. "Where are we?"

"The device is called a jar," someone answered.

"Inescapable," added another.

"Quite true, I'm afraid," said Joule.

"We're all going to die!" wailed the first again.

"Calm down!" Newton pleaded. "You'll deafen me. Let's think... This child... he's using your lanterns to light his way."

"And how could a creature such as this know such a thing?" a fellow captive asked Joule.

"A creature such as this..." Newton sneered. He paused to study the looming face, dreadful and distorted by the curve of the glass but unmistakable. "The Great Designer!"

"What use is such knowledge to us?"

Newton focused. His adventure had used up more electrons than he thought. Brightening was hard work, but he managed a look of importance. "It's your light he wants."

"So you have said."

"So...shut it off." Newton dimmed.

"Joule, your companion has quite lost his mind. Glow on everyone, we must summon help."

"You've got it all backward! Don't you see? More fireflies will only end up in here with us. We have to get the child to let us go."

"How, pray tell?"

"Take away what he wants. Turn your lanterns off."

"Ridiculous."

"Insanity, I'd say."

Newton buzzed about angrily. "It's the only way."

"Calm yourself, tiny friend," said Joule.

"Quit calling me tiny!" Newton snapped. A wave of dizziness overtook him and he tumbled off Joule's back, landing roughly on the outstretched wing of the next firefly down. He looked up into Joule's worried face.

"You look pale my... Newton."

"I'm fine," Newton grumbled, puffing spurts of russet in his effort to climb the antenna Joule offered.

"Attention, everyone!" Joule said to the others. "I believe Newton is right. Put out your lanterns, at once!"

They did.

Nothing happened.

"Did I not tell you?" a voice echoed in the darkness.

"Patience!"

After what seemed like forever, the jar began to shake wildly, sending fireflies sprawling every which way, banging into each other and into the sides of the jar. Newton lost his grip on Joule's antenna and was thrown across the jar. "Joule! Jou..." The beating wing of a panicked firefly slapped Newton senseless. Another terrified beetle clipped him with his antenna, sending him off in another direction altogether, until he slammed into something cold, and very solid. Everything went black.

"Open your eyes, friend Newton. Please."

The words seem to float sweetly through the air like waves of Mother Cathode's offering. Newton tried to open his eyes but found he couldn't. "Wick?"

"I know no one by that name. It is I, Lieutenant Versicolor Joule of..."

The rest of the words were lost to Newton. He felt light-headed. It was all beginning to come back... the Great Designer...the jar...

"Friend Newton, your lantern has all but gone out."

Newton managed to open his eyes enough to see Joule hovering over him. "The others?" he moaned.

"They have all flown."

"What happened?"

"The Great Designer removed the lid and released us, as you predicted."

"Good."

"You, however, were badly injured."

"Me? *Nah.* I'm a tough little speck. I'll be okay." Newton tried to get up. "Why won't the world stand still?"

"*You* need to be still. You are weak, perhaps hungry."

"Hungry..."

"Do pixels not eat?"

"Eat?"

Joule smiled weakly. "Stay here. I shall fix everything." The breeze from Joule's wings as he took off felt good. Watching his friend's familiar dance light a path across the dark sky helped Newton relax. Six quick flashes, a swoop, and a long upward trail of saffron. Six flashes, a swoop, and...

Six more flashes? Someone was dancing with Joule. A swoop, a long upward trail, then the answer. Why did the pattern of the answer seem so familiar? Why couldn't he remember? Something Joule had told him. What?

The truth slammed into Newton every bit as hard as the glass jar. "Joule! Don't let her trick you!" Newton leapt to his feet then stumbled backward. He shook his head, trying to stop it spinning. He had to warn his friend, but how? The light from Joule's dance was so far away. How could he ever get there on his own? The few electrons Newton had left buzzed with effort. Yes! He would turn himself on, pure white, full bright. He focused...

Producing nothing more than a muddy beige hum. When tears threatened to come, Newton curled himself into a ball, squeezing his arms and legs against his square body, tighter and tighter, until he no longer felt the ground beneath his feet.

Because his feet weren't on the ground! He was floating just above it. Holding his focus on staying airborne, slowly, carefully, Newton let himself uncurl. "Take that Lieutenant Smarty-pants! You're not the only one who can fly." Newton drifted higher and higher, leaving the ground far below. "I'm coming, friend," he called, and banked to the left. A little too far, though. He lost his balance and tumbled into a nosedive. The ground spun in circles, growing sickeningly closer with every somersault. Focus, Newton told himself, focus. That only made him fall faster, so he stretched himself out as wide as he could, every finger, every toe spread out to meet the air. He slowed to a stop so close to the ground he could touch it. He kissed it instead, took ten deep breaths, then set off after Joule.

A yellow streak shot across a patch of wet grass below. Six flashes, a swoop, and a rising yellow streak. "Joule!" Six quick flashes, a swoop, and...

No yellow streak. "Joule!" Newton relaxed and let himself drift downward. "Can you hear me, Joule?" Six flashes, a swoop, followed closely by another swoop. It was Lampyridia all right, and she was after his friend. "No, Joule! It's a trick!"

Newton focused; flying faster until he reached where Lampyridia had Joule pinned beneath her on the edge of an elm leaf. She was monstrous, at least twice the size of poor Joule who was struggling frantically to free himself from her evil grasp. What could someone as tiny as Newton do against such a huge and hideous creature?

Of course! He would trick the trickster. Newton turned his very best, very brightest saffron, flashed six times, swooped and rose, flashed, swooped and...

It was no use.

Lampyridia let out a deep-throated cackle and sank her teeth into the back of Joule's neck. Joule's howl of pain froze Newton in his tracks. But not for long. Something inside him short-circuited. Anger overcame weariness and he flung himself at the queen, landing with a wallop against the back of her head, catching her off guard. In a single push, Newton discharged every electron he had left. A blinding flash of white light left his body and crackled down Lampyridia's back in jagged bolts of blue spark. She shuddered and slid off the leaf, taking Joule and Newton along with her, all three crashing to the ground in a tangled pile.

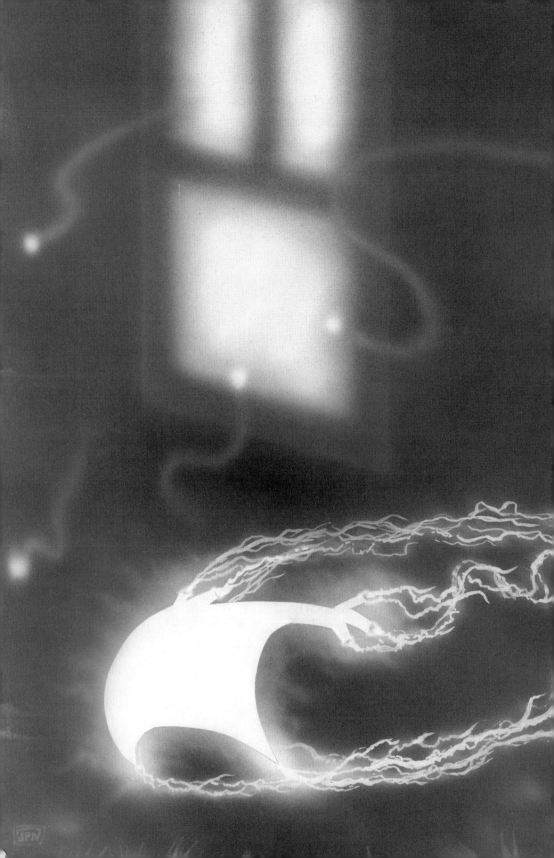

Newton felt as if his head had exploded. He reached up and touched it just to make sure. He slid down off the queen's back and looked up at her black smoldering mass. Her huge green eyes stared back at him. Then she rolled over. Newton gave a little sigh of relief when Joule wriggled out from under her, groaning. "Is she...?"

"She is — dead as a larva's dinner. And as for meals," Joule added, offering Newton an antenna up, "you look ready for yours now more than ever. I shall retrieve it for you."

Newton could feel himself fading fast. He hadn't even realized Joule was gone until he saw him returning with something in his mouth. Newton tried to speak. "What's...that?"

"Supper — fit for a hero."

"What..."

"Catch of the day — mosquito. What I eat when my lantern gets dim."

"What...do...I do?"

"Let me demonstrate." Newton watched Joule bite into the mosquito, pull his mouth away, move his jaws up and down for a moment, then motion to him to try. He couldn't move. Joule looked worried. Newton tried to smile.

"Perhaps you have more of a taste for snail?"

"No...taste...for...anything...but what...Mother... Cathode...feeds me."

"You need to go home then. And I shall take you." Joule extended an antenna. "Come..."

But Newton had no energy to climb. He lay there, flat, exhausted, nearly black.

Joule scratched his head with his antenna, looked at it, brightened, then slipped the antenna into his mouth. He swished it from side to side a few times, then spat it out and touched Newton with it. Newton found himself held to it by something moist and sweet smelling. "Off we go then," said Joule. He spread his magnificent wings and lifted them both into the air.

Newton must have drifted off because the next thing he knew, they were landing on the screen of the grand window across the way, beyond which his own monitor screen radiated a welcoming glow.

"The rest of the journey is up to you, friend pixel. The screen in this window permits air to pass, but alas, not fireflies. You have proven yourself capable of flight. Now go."

Except, no matter how tightly he focused, Newton couldn't even take off. He slipped through the screen and dropped onto the windowsill inside. His friend called to him from what seemed a long way away... something. Newton was too tired to make out what. He heard Joule's wings unfurl and felt the gust of air from his takeoff, the force of which blew his limp body right off the sill.

Downward he fell without making any effort to stop himself, toward the floor behind the Great Designer's chair. Soon he would hit the floor and go out.

Forever.

Something pillowy soft brushed against his sticky body and clung to it. Another gust of breeze from outside caught him and the dust particle that was his new companion, and carried them upward. Newton vaguely thought he heard a small cheer from behind. As he and the dust particle drifted in the direction of the monitor screen, they found themselves drawn toward it more and more. Closer and closer they came, until...

Snap!

Newton's ears popped and suddenly he realized that his arms and legs were pinned to his body. He felt cramped, squashed up against something.

Or someone!

"Newton?"

Wick! He was home! Mother Cathode cycled and Newton greedily gobbled up her offering. He took more than his fair share, but his neighbors didn't mind. They were glad to see him home. But not half as glad as Newton was to *be* home.

"Well! I presume this means you've finally settled on a subject for your project."

His mother's voice startled Danny. He looked up from the brightly colored insect depicted on his computer screen and followed his mother's gaze to the glass jar sitting empty on his desk. "Yeah."

He felt his mother's hand on his shoulder. "Look," she said, nodding toward his bedroom window. A spot of yellow light hovered just beyond the screen, flashed six times, and swooped out of sight.